THE BIRTHDAY LETTERS

By Charlotte Pomerantz
Pictures By JoAnn Adinolfi

Greenwillow Books
An Imprint of HarperCollinsPublishers

For Lysna Scriven-Marzani,
Timothy Carl Nissen,
Harry Schroder
—C. P.

For my dearest niece, Gabrielle,
and for my son, Hans-Liam,
who worked with his mommy
every day on this book. Happy
Birthday to you— May 11, 1999
—J. A.

I painted the illustrations for this book with
watercolors, gouache, and pastel pencils,
in between bites of birthday cake and bits
of letter writing—J. A.

The text type is Korinna.

The Birthday Letters
Text copyright © 2000 by Charlotte Pomerantz
Illustrations copyright © 2000 by JoAnn Adinolfi
Printed in Singapore by Tien Wah Press.
All rights reserved.
http://harperchildrens.com

Library of Congress
Cataloging-in-Publication Data

Pomerantz, Charlotte.
The birthday letters / by Charlotte Pomerantz ;
pictures by JoAnn Adinolfi.
    p.   cm.
"Greenwillow Books."
Summary: When Tom decides to have a birthday
party for his dog Louie, one of the invited guests
unwittingly starts an argument that is carried out
entirely by correspondence.
ISBN 0-688-16335-1 (trade).
ISBN 0-688-16336-X (lib. bdg.)
[1. Letters—Fiction.   2. Birthdays—Fiction.
3. Parties—Fiction.   4. Dogs—Fiction.]
I. Adinolfi, JoAnn, ill.   II. Title.   PZ7.P77Bi
2000   [E]—dc21   98-50914   CIP   AC

10 9 8 7 6 5 4 3 2 1
First Edition

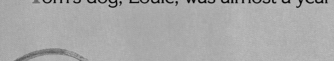
Tom's dog, Louie, was almost a year old.

Tom decided to give him
a birthday party. He wanted
to invite his friends Lily and
Pedro and Pedro's little sister,
Emilia.

His mother and father said he could have a birthday cake.
"Good," said Tom. "Should the invitations come from me—or from Louie?"
"From Louie," said his father and mother.
Tom sat down and wrote,

Dear Lily,

Please come to my birthday party this Saturday at 2 o'clock.
You can bring a dog biscuit or a rubber bone if you want to.

Your friend,

Louie

Tom wrote the same invitation to Pedro and to his little sister, Emilia.

He put one invitation under Lily's door.

He put the others under the door of Pedro and Emilia.

Lily called. She said she could come.

Pedro called. He could come too.
"What about your little sister?"
asked Tom.
"Hold on," said Pedro.
He turned to his sister.
"Tell him I'm writing him a letter,"
said Emilia.
"A letter? Okay," said Tom.

Pedro turned to his sister. "Emilia,
when did you learn how to write?"
"I didn't," said Emilia. "I'm only
in kindergarten, remember?"
She handed Pedro a pencil.
"Write this."

Dear Tom,
Thank you for your
invitation. I will be
there on Saturday
at 2 o'clock with
my gerbils.
    Yours truly,
E m i l i a

Later that day Emilia saw a letter under her door.
She asked Pedro to read it for her.
Pedro read,

Dear Emilia,
This is a party for Louie.
Do not bring your gerbils.

Tom
on behalf of Louie

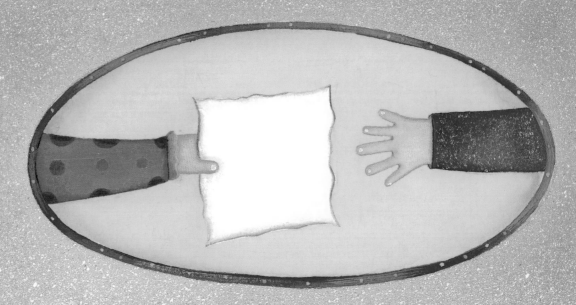

"Pedro," said Emilia, "this calls for a reply."
She handed him a piece of paper.
"Write this," she said.

Dear Tom,
We are very small and
we won't eat much
birthday cake.

E m i l i a

on behalf of the gerbils

Tom took the letter and headed downstairs
to Pedro and Emilia's apartment.

He knocked loudly on the door.
Emilia answered the door.

"N-O," said Tom. "That spells <u>no</u>.
No gerbils are invited to Louie's party."

Emilia sucked in her breath.
"I know what N-O spells.
I also know that you're the
meanest Potato-head
in the whole world!"

She slammed the door with a bang.

The next morning Pedro saw
a letter under the door
addressed to Emilia.
"Did you read it?" she asked.
"Of course not," said Pedro.
"It was addressed to you."
Emilia took the letter and
opened it. She handed it
back to Pedro. "Now you
can read it," she said.
Pedro read,

Dear Emilia,

You are N-O-T spells <u>not</u> invited to my birthday party.

Louie

P.S. I only invited you because you are Pedro's little sister.

P.P.S. Gerbils give me the willies.

"Grrr," said Emilia.
Pedro sighed and
picked up a pencil.

Dear Louie,
Did you write that letter—or did Tom write it?
Tom is a mean Potato-head but you are a nice dog.
So may I please come to your
birthday party?
Your friend (I hope),

E m i l i a

Emilia met Tom on the way to school. She handed
him the letter.
Tom started to open it.
"The letter is N-O-T spells <u>not</u> for you," said Emilia.
"It's for Louie."
"Oh," said Tom. He put it in his pocket.

When Emilia came home, there was another letter
under the door. She opened it and looked at it.
"I'll save it for when Pedro comes home."

That night, when she lay in bed,
Emilia remembered the letter.
She handed it to Pedro in the
upper bunk bed.
"Read it, please," she said.
Pedro leaned over the bunk
and read,

Dear Emilia,

It so happens that I am a D-O-G
who can write. And I ~~defnitly~~
don't want you to come to my
birthday party.

Louie

"What's crossed out?" said Emilia.
"The word <u>definitely</u>," said Pedro.
"He must have had trouble
spelling it."

Pedro sighed. "I wonder why Louie doesn't like you.
He always wags his tail when he sees you."
The room was very quiet.

"It's Potato-head who doesn't like me," said Emilia. "He's just <u>pretending</u> it's Louie." She sat up. "I'm not going to let Potato-head stop me."
"What are you going to do?" said Pedro.
"I don't know yet, but I'll find a way," said Emilia.

It was the day of Louie's birthday party.
Tom gave Louie a rubber bone. Lily gave him
a ball. Pedro gave him some dog biscuits.
Lily was about to light the birthday candle
when the doorbell rang.

In walked Emilia. She was dressed
in a long party dress and sneakers.
"What are you doing here!" said Tom.
Before Emilia could answer, Louie
ran over to her. He began jumping
up and down.

"Happy birthday, Louie," said Emilia.
"Come here, Louie," ordered Tom.
But Louie kept on jumping.
"Look at him," said Lily.
"He can't stop jumping."

Tom grabbed the dog by the collar.
"Emilia," he said, "you were <u>not</u>
invited to my party."
"It's not your party,"
said Emilia. "It's Louie's party."
"So what!" shouted Tom.
"It's my house."
"Chill," said Emilia.
"I just came by to say
happy birthday to Louie."

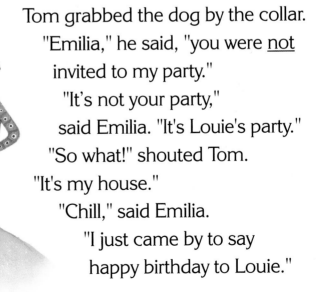

Suddenly Louie broke away from Tom and jumped all over Emilia again.

Lily said, "What's going on, Louie? You've never been this way before."
She turned to Tom.
"Look at Louie. That dog is crazy about Emilia."
Tom looked at Louie.
Then he looked at Emilia.
"Something is fishy," he said.
Louie kept on jumping.
"Look how happy he is," said Lily. "Why can't Emilia stay?"

Tom shrugged. "All right," he said. "Emilia can stay. But I still say something is fishy."

When no one was looking,
Emilia sneaked into the kitchen.
Louie followed.

She took a gift-
wrapped package
out of her pocket.

She tore open the paper
    and pulled out a big steak bone.

She gave the bone to Louie
and said, "Good idea, huh?"

That night, before they went to
sleep, Emilia said to Pedro,
"Louie's birthday party was lots
of fun. I think I'll give a party for
my gerbils." She handed Pedro
a piece of paper and a pencil.
"Please write this," she said.

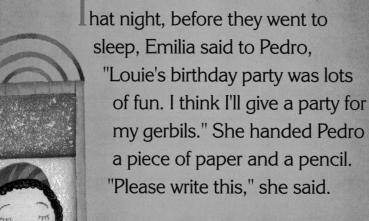

The End